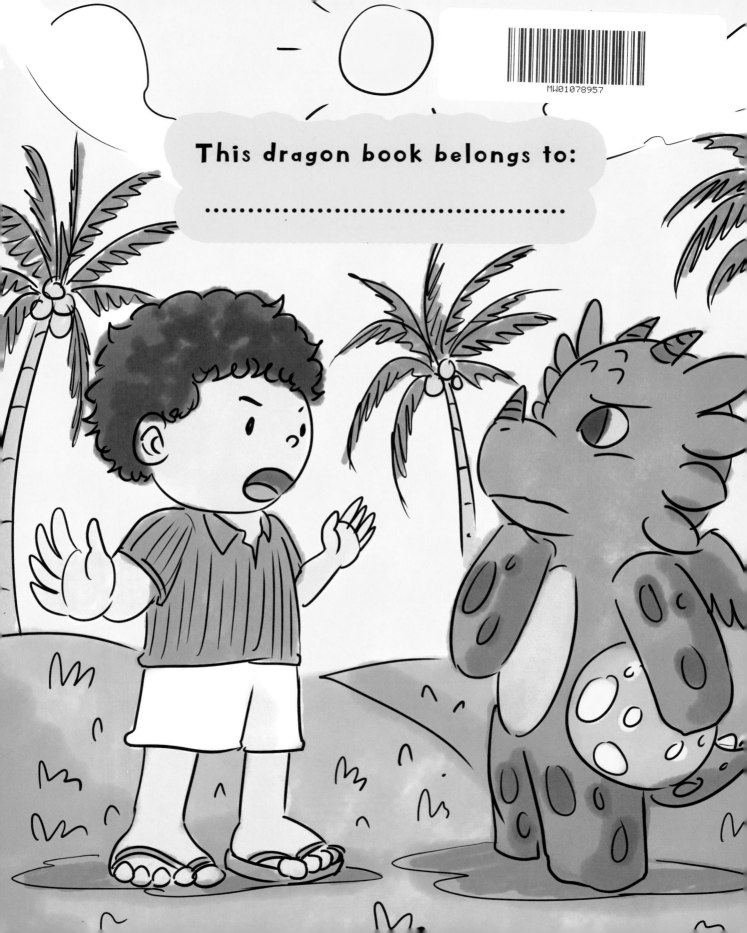

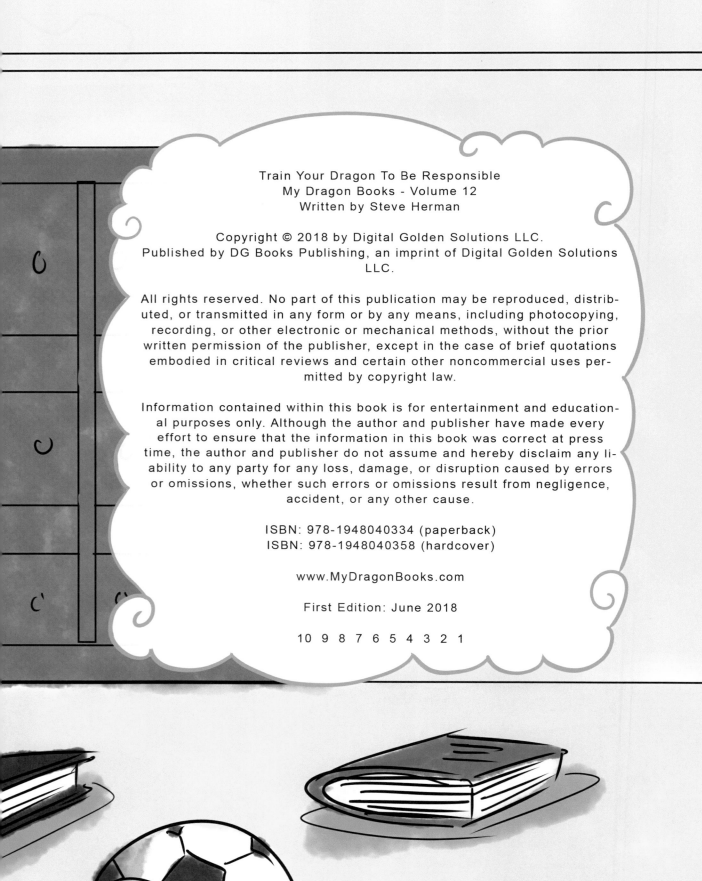

Train Your Dragon To Be Responsible
My Dragon Books - Volume 12
Written by Steve Herman

ISBN: 978-1948040334 (paperback)
ISBN: 978-1948040358 (hardcover)

www.MyDragonBooks.com

First Edition: June 2018

10 9 8 7 6 5 4 3 2 1

Train Your Dragon To Be Responsible

My Dragon Books - Volume 12

Steve Herman

Hello! My name is Drew;
I have a dragon for a pet,
And that's about as cool a pet
as anyone can get!

His name is Diggory Doo,
and he doesn't scratch or bite –
For a prehistoric creature,
he's really quite polite.

A dragon's not too tough to train;
it takes no time at all –
Just have a little patience,
and start when he is small.

Diggory used to wake up late
and miss the bus to school;
He tried to place the blame on me,
which isn't very cool.

"It's not my fault at all," he cried. "I tried my very best! YOU didn't wake me up, so I couldn't get up and get dressed!"

Another time when Diggory Doo
would not accept the blame
Was when he lost his temper,
and he breathed a little flame.

Dad's favorite chair went up
in smoke before we even knew it –
"You made me mad," said Diggory Doo.
"That's what made me do it!"

And all the words came tumbling out when he should hold them back – "That's just how I am," he cried, "A talking maniac!"

Mother baked a chocolate cake, but when it was finished cooking, Diggory ate it all himself when no one else was looking.

"Don't be mad," said Diggory Doo,
"You know cake is yummy;
That is why I could not wait
to get it in my tummy!"

Sometimes Diggory skipped his chores to watch some television - He'd not admit even a bit it was a bad decision.

"Perhaps your viewing time," I said,
"could use some limitation."
"Don't blame me," said Diggory Doo.
"I can't resist temptation!"

Diggory teased a boy in class;
teacher sent him home from school,
Cause that's what teachers do
when dragons choose to break a rule.

"It's not my fault," yelled Diggory Doo,
"when I did something bad;
I'd not have done it,
if he didn't make me so mad!"

"It's not my fault!" he'd always say
whenever he had blown it –
I told him when he messes up,
he really ought to own it.

Now you set your own alarm
so you're never late to school,

And when you're mad,
you count to ten and let your temper cool.

You've learned to practice self control
so you can do what's right
Like wait your turn to speak
and not eat cakes in just one bite.

You turn the TV off
until you've done what you must do,
And you're careful what you say,
no matter what's been said to you.

"Now I'm much more careful
of the choices that I make,
And I carefully consider
all the chances that I take."

"We all make mistakes," I said.
"We've all committed wrongs -
When you make a poor decision,
place the blame where it belongs."

Whenever you've done something that you really ought not do, Don't put the blame on someone else; admit that it was you.

Then next time when you're tempted
to do what you should not,
You'll remember how that felt
and the lesson that it taught.

POTTY TRAIN YOUR DRAGON
Steve Herman

TRAIN YOUR ANGRY DRAGON
Steve Herman

THE MINDFUL DRAGON
Steve Herman

THE YOGA DRAGON
Steve Herman

DRAGON & THE BULLY
Steve Herman

HAPPY BIRTHDAY DRAGON
Steve Herman

TRAIN YOUR DRAGON TO ACCEPT NO
Steve Herman

I GOT THIS!
Steve Herman

TRAIN YOUR DRAGON TO BE KIND
Steve Herman

A DRAGON With His Mouth ON FIRE
Steve Herman

TRAIN YOUR DRAGON To Follow RULES
Steve Herman

TRAIN YOUR DRAGON To Be RESPONSIBLE
Steve Herman

TRAIN YOUR DRAGON To LOVE HIMSELF
Steve Herman

TRAIN YOUR DRAGON To Understand CONSEQUENCES
Steve Herman

TEACH YOUR DRAGON TO STOP LYING
Steve Herman

TEACH YOUR DRAGON TO MAKE FRIENDS
Steve Herman

TEACH YOUR DRAGON TO SHARE
Steve Herman

FIX YOUR DRAGON'S ATTITUDE
Steve Herman

GET YOUR DRAGON TO TRY NEW THINGS
Steve Herman

TEACH YOUR DRAGON TO FOLLOW INSTRUCTIONS
Steve Herman

A DRAGON CHRISTMAS
Steve Herman

HELP YOUR DRAGON DEAL WITH ANXIETY
Steve Herman

TEACH YOUR DRAGON MANNERS
Steve Herman

TEACH YOUR DRAGON EMPATHY
Steve Herman

TEACH YOUR DRAGON About DIVERSITY
Steve Herman

HELP YOUR DRAGON
Learn From **MISTAKES**
Steve Herman

HELP YOUR DRAGON
DEAL WITH **CHANGE**
Steve Herman

THE **SAD DRAGON**
A DRAGON BOOK ABOUT GRIEF AND LOSS
Steve Herman

DRAGON
SIBLING RIVALRY
Steve Herman

LIMIT YOUR DRAGON'S
SCREEN TIME
Steve Herman

DRAGON and **HIS FRIEND**
A Dragon Book About Autism
Steve Herman

TEACH YOUR DRAGON
GOOD **HYGIENE**
Steve Herman

TEACH YOUR DRAGON
ABOUT **STRANGER DANGER**
Steve Herman

HELP YOUR DRAGON
COPE WITH **TRAUMA**
Steve Herman

HELP YOUR DRAGON
OVERCOME **SEPARATION ANXIETY**
Steve Herman

TRAIN YOUR DRAGON
TO DO **HARD THINGS**
Steve Herman

TWO HOMES
FILLED WITH **LOVE**
Steve Herman

DRAGON'S MASK
Steve Herman

VIRTUAL LEARNING
DRAGON
Steve Herman

THE **FOSTER**
DRAGON
Steve Herman

A DRAGON
WITH **ADHD**
Steve Herman

GET YOUR DRAGON
TO EAT **HEALTHY FOOD**
Steve Herman

TEACH YOUR DRAGON
RESPECT
Steve Herman

TEACH YOUR DRAGON
BODY SAFETY
Steve Herman

THE **BOSSY**
DRAGON
Steve Herman

TEACH YOUR DRAGON
INTEGRITY
Steve Herman

BE A **GOOD SPORT**
DIGGORY DOO!
Steve Herman

A DRAGON
NEEDS HIS **SLEEP**
Steve Herman

A DRAGON
HAS TO **PERSEVERE**
Steve Herman

CELEBRATE
OUR **DIFFERENCES**
Steve Herman

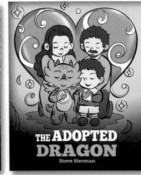

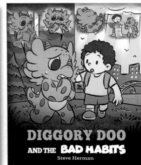

Made in United States
Troutdale, OR
10/14/2023

13708496R00026